CHICO BON BON AND THE EGG-MERGENCY!

Adapted by Tina Gallo
Episode written by Halcyon Person
Based on the TV show *Chico Bon Bon: Monkey with a Tool Belt*

SIMON SPOTLIGHT
New York London Toronto Sydney New Delhi

SIMON SPOTLIGHT

An imprint of Simon & Schuster Children's Publishing Division

1230 Avenue of the Americas, New York, New York 10020

This Simon Spotlight edition December 2021

CHICO BON BON™ MONKEY WITH A TOOL BELT™ Chico Bon Bon: Monkey with a Tool Belt Copyright © 2021 Monkey WTB Limited, a Silvergate Media company. All rights reserved.

All rights reserved, including the right of reproduction in whole or in part in any form.

SIMON SPOTLIGHT, and colophon are registered trademarks of Simon & Schuster, Inc.

For information about special discounts for bulk purchases, please contact Simon & Schuster Special Sales at 1-866-506-1949 or business@simonandschuster.com.

Manufactured in the United States of America 1021 LAK

2 4 6 8 10 9 7 5 3 1

ISBN 978-1-6659-0482-7

ISBN 978-1-6659-0483-4 (ebook)

One beautiful morning in Blunderburg, Clark noticed that Chico Bon Bon and Rainbow Thunder were carrying a large box. Clark asked what was inside.

Chico smiled. "We are getting ready to have a **DANCE PARTY**," he said. "Our new **DISCO BALL** just came in the mail!"

"Oh! I'd better get ready to boogie!" Clark said, and he showed off a dance move.

Clark's dance move knocked the box right out of his friends' hands. The box bounced against the wall, and slammed onto the floor.

"**OH NO!**" Clark said sadly. "I'm so clumsy! The disco ball is made of glass. It must have broken into a million pieces."

"Don't worry," Chico said. "The disco ball is fine!"

He took it out of the box to show Clark.

Clark was shocked. "But . . . how?" he asked.

"This box was designed with **SHOCK ABSORPTION** in mind," Rainbow Thunder said.

"It's full of these **SUPER SQUISHY** packing peanuts," she explained.

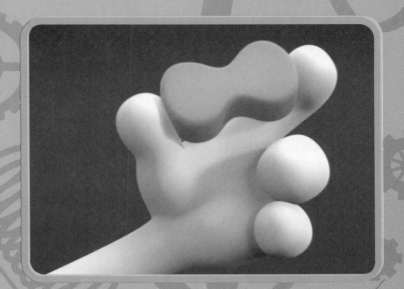

"When something fragile like a disco ball falls to the ground, the energy goes from the disco ball into the packing peanuts, so the disco ball doesn't break," Rainbow Thunder continued. "It's called **SHOCK ABSORPTION!**"

"Shock absorption! That's nuts!" Clark cheered. "*Pea-nuts*, that is! These are perfect for my peanut collection." Clark took a handful of packing peanuts to keep.

Just then the BANANA PHONE RANG! Chico answered it. "Chico Bon Bon. Got a problem? We can solve 'em!"

It was Neil and Nell Ostrich on the phone with a big announcement. Their **EGG** was about to **HATCH**, and they needed a way to get it safely to the hatchery right away!

"We need the Fix-It Force," Neil said.

"Neil, Nell, this problem is no problem," Chico Bon Bon said. "Fix-It Force, it's time to bring the awesome!"

The Fix-It Force piled into Tool Force One with Neil, Nell, and their egg.

"Let's get this egg to Hatchery Hospital **FAST**," Chico said.

Nell Ostrich told the group that the egg had to be kept warm. "No problem," Chico said. "We'll put it in Clark's bubble. It's climate-controlled, so it will stay nice and warm."

But when Chico gave the egg to Clark, Clark almost dropped it. "I'm so clumsy!" Clark cried. He was worried he'd accidentally hurt the egg.

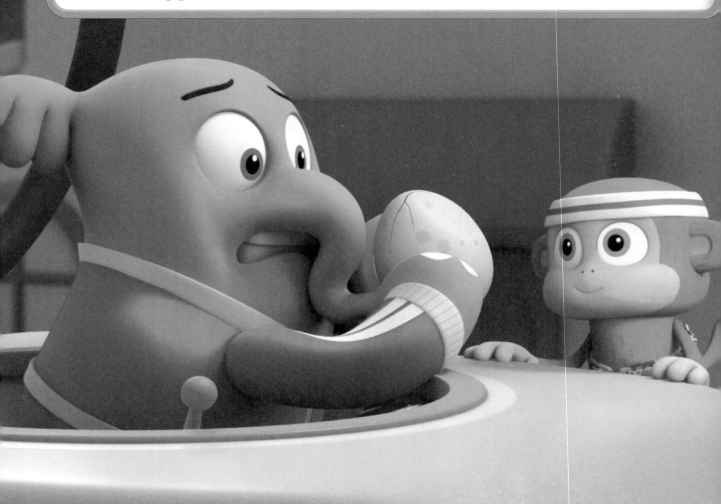

Chico taped the egg to Clark's chest, so the egg was safe and warm. Then the group encountered another problem: **JACKHAMMER JUNCTION**!

"This road's too bumpy! If we drive through there, the egg will break!" Clark cried.

"We need some shock absorbing materials," Rainbow Thunder said. "Something **SOFT** and **SQUISHY** to protect the egg."

"I've got it!" Chico said. "**BALLOONS** are super soft and squishy!"

They filled Clark's bubble with balloons.

"Don't worry, little Eggy," Clark said. "These balloons will absorb any shocks and keep you safe!"

The balloons kept the egg safe through Jackhammer Junction. But Rainbow Thunder hit a big bump, and all the balloons popped!

Now they needed something else for shock absorption, as they were about to go through **WRECKING BALL BOULEVARD**!

The Fix-It Force was out of balloons, so they needed something else soft and squishy. "MARSHMALLOWS!" Chico said. "They are super soft and squishy. Just what we need."

"Marshmallows are my favorite!" Clark said. He smiled at the egg. "You are going to love them too, Eggy!"

The marshmallows stayed soft and squishy, cushioning the egg as they drove on Wrecking Ball Boulevard! But Clark loved marshmallows, and all the excitement made him hungry. So he ate all of them!

Now the Fix-It Force needed something else to protect the egg—and they needed it fast—since they were about to go through **BURPY BIRD PARK**!

"Their burps make the ground jiggle like jelly," Rainbow Thunder said.

"That's it!" Chico said. "We can use **JELLY** for shock absorption! But I have to use a jelly that Clark won't want to eat." Chico set his mega-tool to spray pistachio jelly into Clark's bubble. Clark did not like pistachios!

The jelly kept the egg safe, and they made it to the hospital in time, but soon they had another problem. The Egg-mergency room was on the top floor of the hospital—and the elevator was broken!

"The fastest way to get the egg to the Egg-mergency room is through a chute on the roof," Rainbow Thunder said.

"Clark, can you take the **CLARKCOPTER** to the roof?" Chico asked.

Clark was suddenly very nervous. "Me? Are you sure?" he asked.

"Don't worry, I'll be with you every step of the way," Chico promised, so Clark agreed to do it.

At first, Clark almost dropped the egg, but he caught it just in the nick of time.

Chico sent Clark a message over the video screen. "Don't give up, Clark!" Chico cheered. "You can do this!"

"Yes! I can do this! For **YOU**, Eggy!" Clark cried, as he flew the Clarkcopter to the roof.

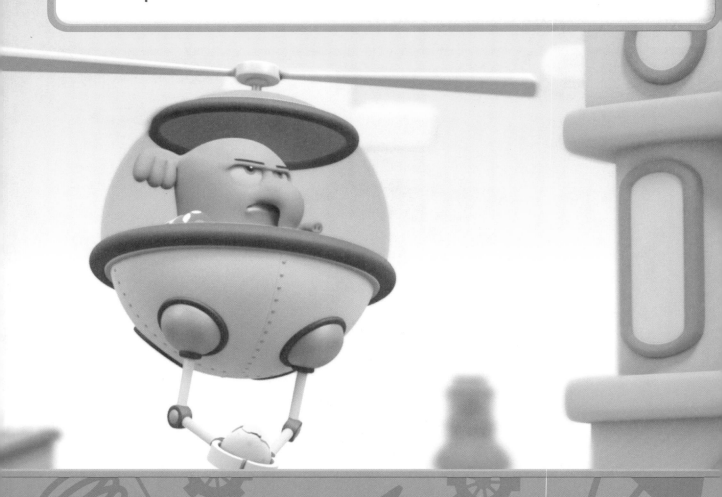

Clark had to drop the egg down the chute **WITHOUT BREAKING IT**. He wasn't sure how to do it, so he took a peanut break! After his snack, Clark realized that he could cushion the egg with the packing peanuts he had saved from the disco ball's box. He carefully covered the egg in packing peanuts. It was already starting to hatch!

"Don't you worry, little Eggy," Clark said. He carefully dropped the egg down the chute!

The egg landed safely in the Egg-mergency room and hatched safely in Hatchery Hospital! Everyone was there to greet Baby Ostrich Nina, thanks to the Fix-It Force!

"**WELCOME TO THE WORLD, BABY NINA!**" said Clark.

BABY OSTRICH IS ON BOARD!

Neil and Nell Ostrich need help from Chico Bon Bon and the Fix-It Force to bring their egg to the Hatchery Hospital before it hatches! The Fix-It Force takes the egg and Ostriches through Blunderburg in Tool Force One, using balloons, marshmallows, and pudding to cushion the egg and deliver it safely.

ADAPTED BY TINA GALLO
EPISODE WRITTEN BY HALCYON PERSON

**LOOK FOR MORE BOOKS ABOUT
CHICO BON BON AT YOUR FAVORITE STORE!**

Visit us at
SIMONANDSCHUSTER.COM/KIDS

SIMON SPOTLIGHT
Simon & Schuster, New York
CHICO BON BON™ MONKEY WITH A TOOL BELT™ Chico Bon Bon:
Monkey with a Tool Belt Copyright © 2021 Monkey WTB Limited, a
Silvergate Media company. All rights reserved.
chicobonbonseries.com

ISBN 978-1-6659-0482-7 $4.99 U.S./$6.99 Can.

EBOOK EDITION ALSO AVAILA

1221

50499